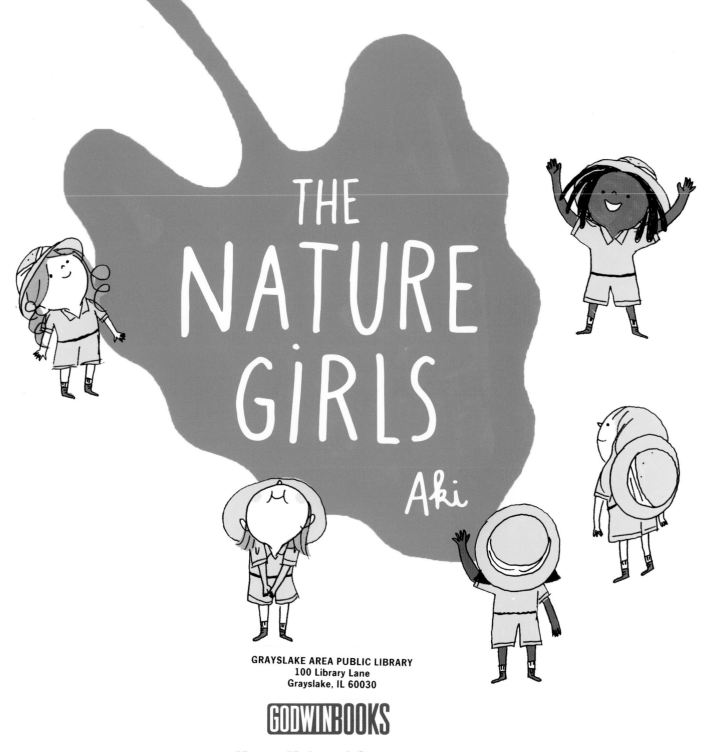

THE NATURE GIRLS

Aki

GODWIN BOOKS

Henry Holt and Company

New York

MEET THE NATURE GIRLS

Sarah

Cathleen

Lucy

Zoe

Kirsten

Tilly

Joy

Emily

We're Nature Girls! We must explore.
We pack our bags, we're out the door . . .

. . . and off we go! There's much to see.
We'll start our journey by the sea.

A pod of dolphins
swims nearby.
The fish come, too.
We all say hi!

It's time to go.
We march along.
We smile at birds
and share their song.

On we trek, across the land.
Up ahead, we see some sand!

A camel pads up to our side.
He takes us for a bumpy ride.

In tall grass, we creep up—slow.
All around are buffalo.

See ya, plains! It's been nice!
Now we're off to find some *ice*!

A tawny owl! She sees us, too.

She hoots a question: "Whooo are you?"

The tundra has snow everywhere.
Look how cute—an Arctic hare!

There's one more stop on our big trip.
We've got our compass and our ship!

The forest's lush and filled with sound. Look at all this life we've found!

It's hard to leave, but we must go.
There's more to see
and do
and know.

MEET THE BIOMES

A **BIOME** is a community of plants and animals that covers a large area of the earth. The climate—how hot or cold it is, how much rain or snowfall there is (as measured over a long period of time)—helps determine what kinds of plants and animals can live in that area.

AQUATIC

Salt water or fresh water, there are so many plants and creatures that live below the surface. Water covers nearly three quarters of the earth's surface—there's a lot to explore!

DESERT

Deserts are dry. There isn't much rain—no more than ten inches a year. In many deserts, days are very hot, and nights are very cold.

 # GRASSLAND

Grasslands are covered with grasses! There aren't many trees. It does rain some—more than in a desert but less than in a forest. Many animals are grazers—grass eaters!

TUNDRA

The tundra is the coldest. No trees live here. There is a thick layer of frozen ground called permafrost. Not many animals live here year round.

 # FOREST

Forests are full of trees and other woody plants. They get more rain than other biomes. There are lots of different kinds of animals.

Henry Holt and Company

Publishers since 1866

Henry Holt® is a registered trademark of Macmillan Publishing Group, LLC

175 Fifth Avenue, New York, NY 10010

mackids.com

Copyright © 2019 by Aki

Library of Congress Control Number: 2018945028

ISBN 978-1-62779-621-7

Our books may be purchased in bulk for promotional, educational, or business use.
Please contact your local bookseller or the Macmillan Corporate and Premium
Sales Department at (800) 221-7945 ext. 5442 or by e-mail at MacmillanSpecialMarkets@macmillan.com.

First edition, 2019 / Designed by Rebecca Syracuse

Printed in China by RR Donnelley Printing Solutions Ltd., Dongguan City, Guangdong Province

1 3 5 7 9 10 8 6 4 2